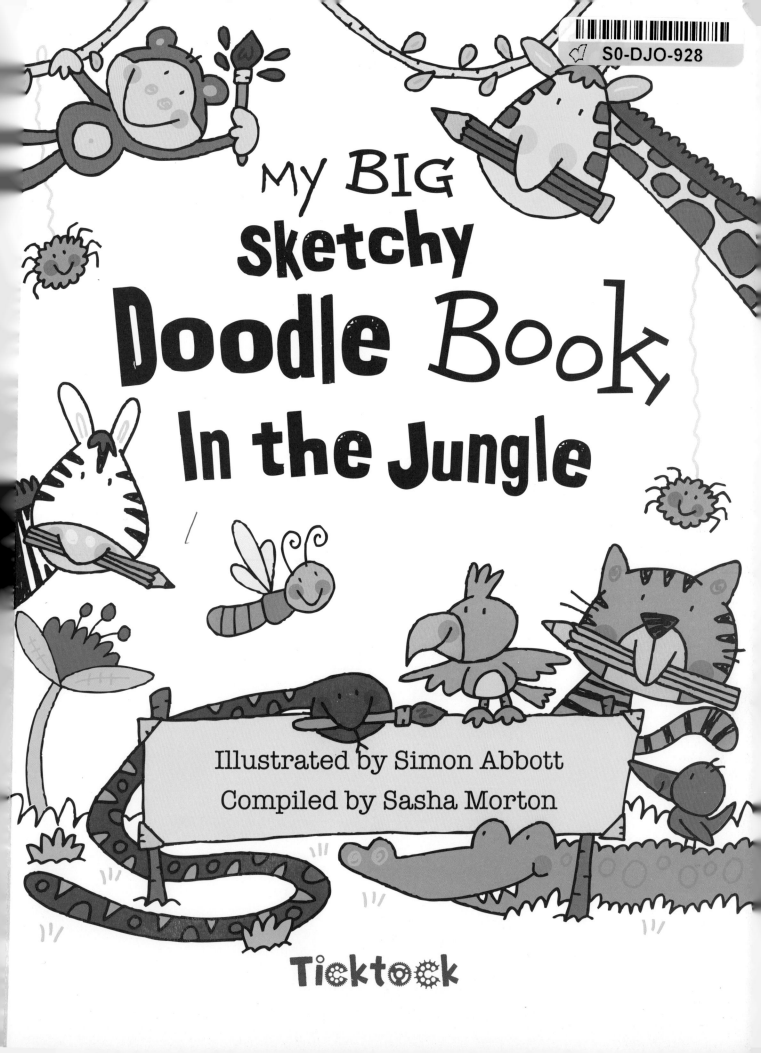

My BIG sketchy Doodle Book In the Jungle

Illustrated by Simon Abbott

Compiled by Sasha Morton

Ticktock

An Hachette UK Company
www.hachette.co.uk

First published in the USA in 2013 by Ticktock,
an imprint of Octopus Publishing Group Ltd,
Endeavour House,
189 Shaftesbury Avenue,
London WC2H 8JY.

www.octopusbooks.co.uk
www.octopusbooksusa.com

Distributed in the US by Hachette Book Group USA
237 Park Avenue, New York,
NY 10017, USA

Distributed in Canada by Canadian Manda Group
165 Dufferin Street, Toronto, Ontario,
Canada, M6K 3H6

ISBN 978 1 84898 851 4

Printed and bound in China
1 3 5 7 9 10 8 6 4 2

Publisher: Tim Cook   Managing editor: Jo Bourne
Project editor: Sasha Morton   Designer: Simon Abbott
Prepress manager: John Lingham   Production controller: Peter Hunt

This book has been filled in by

....

I am ....years old
and my favorite jungle animal is

....

This is what
I look like!

You are off on a jungle adventure.

Color the things you are taking with you.

Add heads to these eyes!

Follow the maze into the jungle.

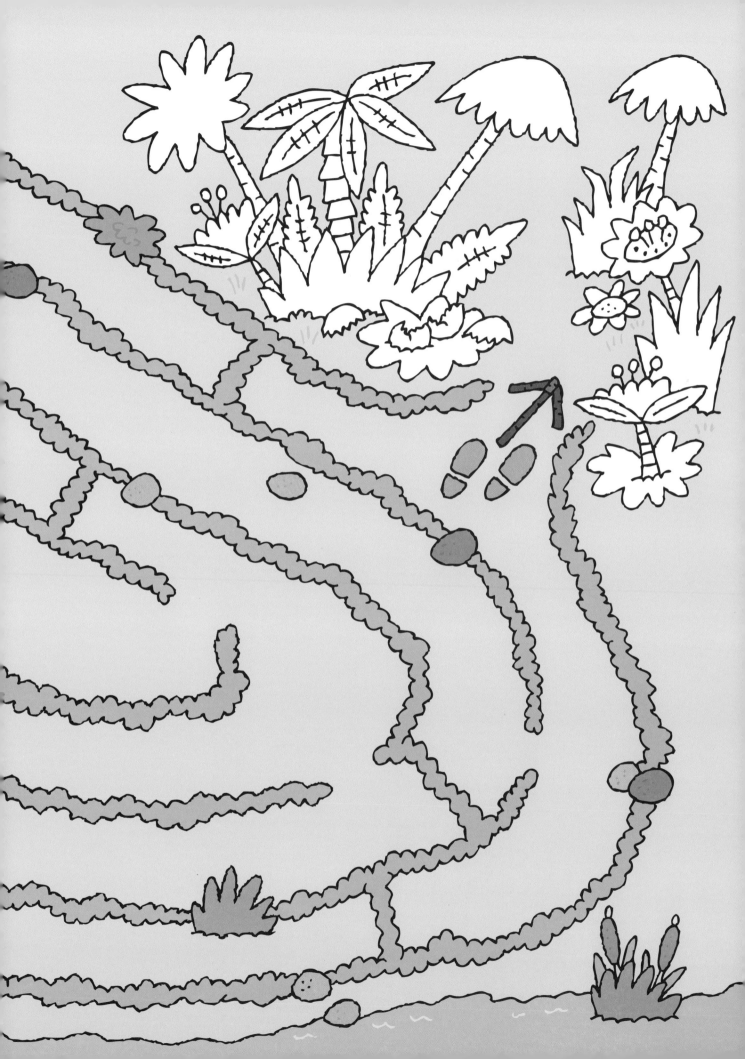

What has hatched?

Draw a creature for each set of footprints.

Fill these pages
with more monkeys
and their bananas.

How many parrots can you spot?

Use your brightest colors to fill in these feathers.

Match the front to the back of each animal.

Now finish them off here!

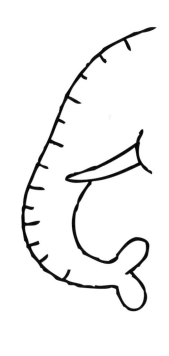

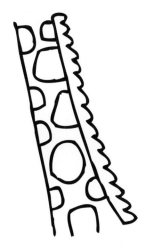

Hiss! Color these snake patterns.

Draw your own scary snakes here.

Who else is hanging out at
the jungle waterfall?

Add more animals to this scene.

Draw a feather headdress
on yourself.

Design a bag made from things you have collected in the jungle.

Color the lizards.

How many can you find?

Finish off these wings with a FANTASTIC pattern.

Climb a tree.

What can you see?

It's time to eat!

What's on your leaf plate?

How many giraffes are there?

Draw the rest of their heads and bodies!

Connect the dots to complete the creature.

Color the rest of the jungle insects.

Draw the reflections of these hippos in the water.

Complete this herd of elephants.

Finish off and color these fabulous jungle plants and flowers.

You find a tree house. What does it look like?

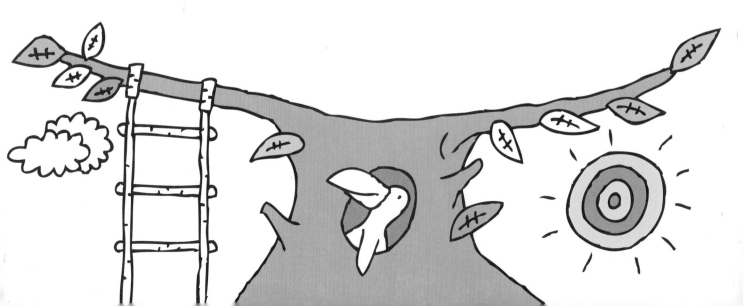

What can you see from your tree house window?

Design a flag to fly from the roof of your tree house.

A cheeky chimp steals your hat!

What does she look like wearing it?

Now give her friends some clothes to wear.

These baby crocodiles are lost.
Can you help them creep
to safety?

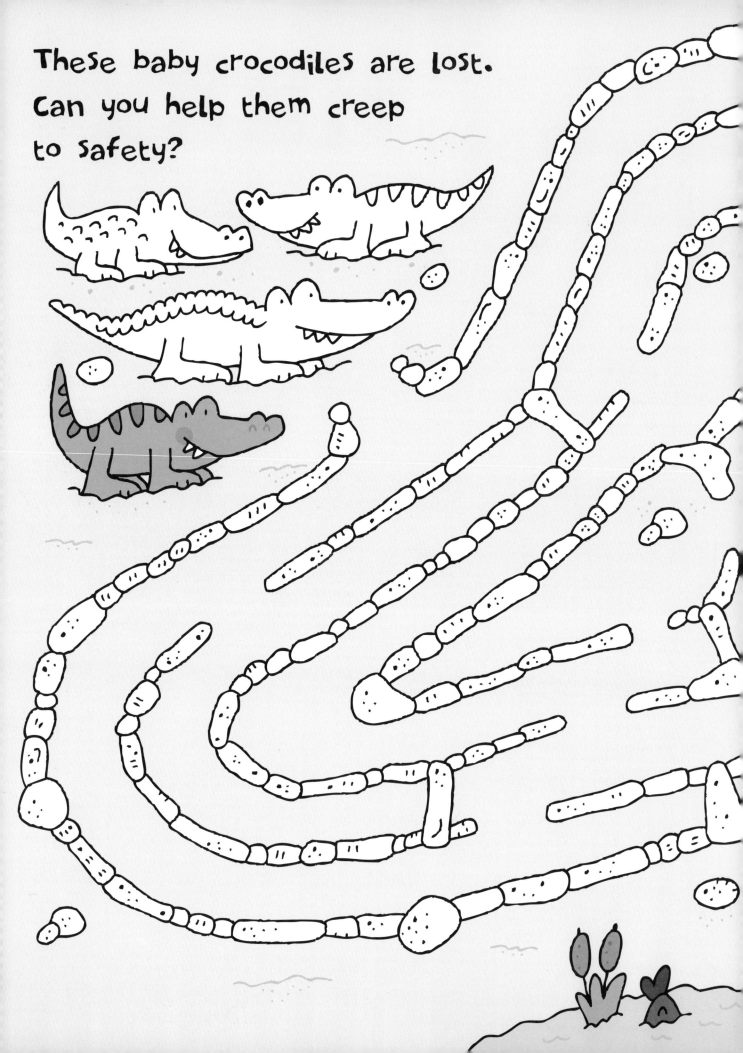

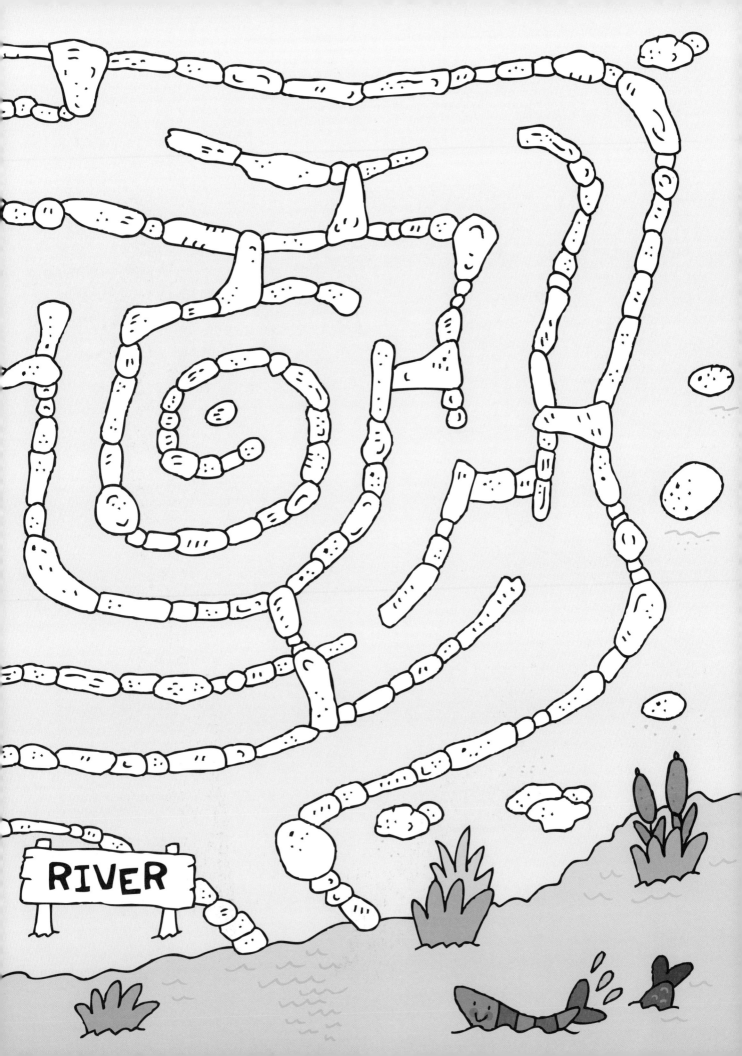

RIVER

These zebras
have lost
their stripes.
Draw them in.

Now put the spots back on these leopards!

You find a cave.
What could be in it?

Color the chameleons. Can you make them disappear?

You decide to make a map of the jungle.

Draw it here.

The sun is going down in the jungle.

Draw the amazing sunset.

You set up camp.
Add a fire, your sleeping bag, and a tent to this scene.

Amazing jungle creatures
come out at night.
What can you see in the
moonlight?

How many bats are in the trees?

Fill *the* page with more bats
in different colors.

Finish off this BEAUTIFUL peacock.

Copy these lions,
using the grid to help you.

You go for a swim in the river.

What can you see under the water?

You discover a lost jungle tribe!
Add more people to their village.

How many people are here now?

Complete the totem pole...

...and color it in.

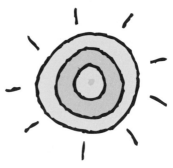

Design
your own
totem pole
here.

Look up high. What's in the sky?

Whose footprints are these
on the riverbank?
Draw in the creature.

Match each animal to its baby.

Now draw them together here.

Gorillas

Crocodiles

Parrots

Tree Frogs

Sloth Bears

Orangutans

The tribe makes a rug for your tree house.
Finish off the pattern.

Now design your own rug here.

Wings or legs? Draw them on.

Complete the picture on the blank puzzle pieces.

What's on the end of your fishing line?

Color the butterfly's wings...

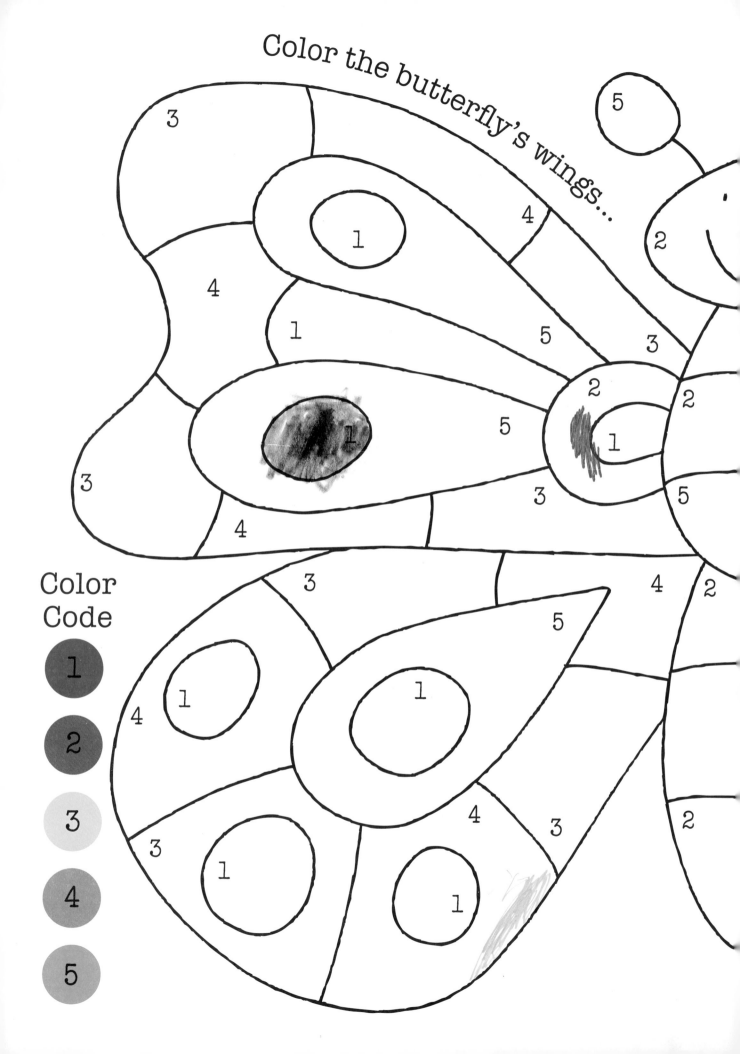

Color Code

1
2
3
4
5

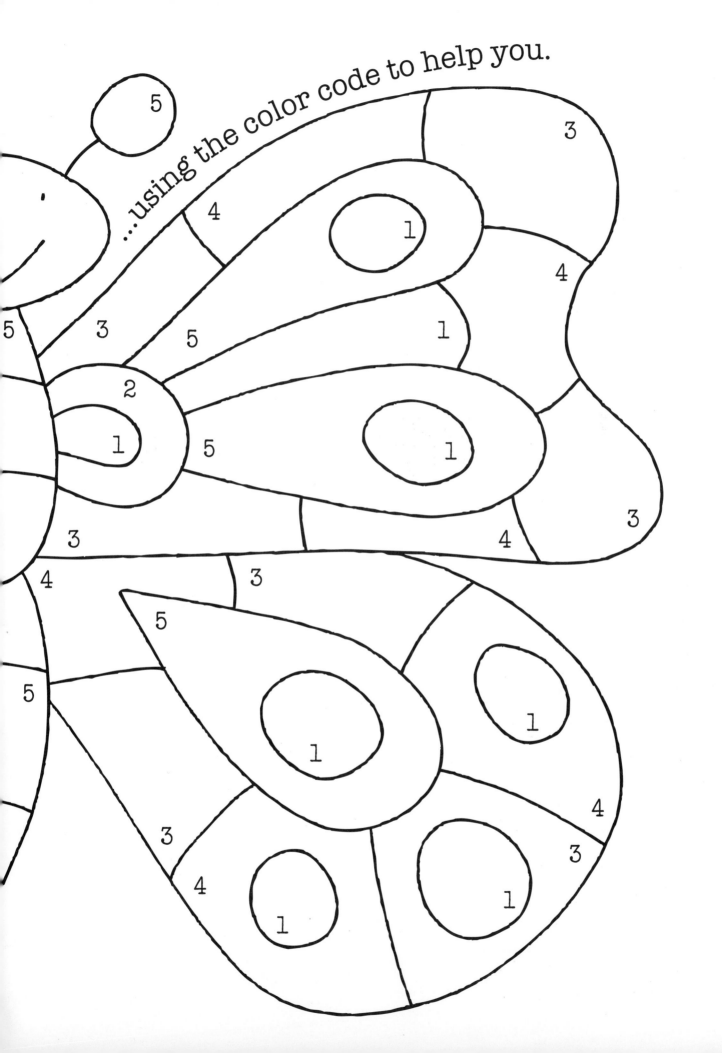

...using the color code to help you.

Fill the page with more plants, flowers, and trees.

It's time to leave the jungle.
Will you travel home by boat, plane,
or even hot air balloon?

MY BIG JUNGLE ADVENTURE

Draw a picture of all of your jungle friends here!

Come back to visit us in the jungle soon!